Strategy
On the
Internet

Shanaya Stephens

Strangers On the Internet

Copyright © 2024 Shanaya Stephens
All rights reserved

The characters and events portrayed in this book are fictitious. Any similarity to real persons, living or dead, is coincidental and not intended by the author.

No part of this book may be reproduced, or stored in a retrieval system, or transmitted in any form or by any means, electronic, mechanical, photocopying, recording, or otherwise, without express written permission of the publisher.

Shanaya Stephens

To,
the internet and the people on it

Subtle author's note:
Also,
If we are related, please do not read this book. I am a nice person, but you will have ideas about me

Disclaimer

This book is a work of fiction. Any resemblances between any person, place, community, entity, cult, country, or religion are purely coincidental. It doesn't aim to condemn, or harm the beliefs of any community, culture, sect, cult, or religion.

Trigger Warning: <u>NOT ADVISED FOR PEOPLE UNDER 18 YEARS OF AGE</u>

This book contains graphic and disturbing content, including suicide, sexual assault, self-harm, domestic violence, childhood abuse, and predatory behaviour over the internet. These themes are portrayed in a realistic and raw manner, and may be triggering for some readers.

Reader discretion is advised. If you are sensitive to these topics or have experienced trauma related to them, please proceed with caution. This book may not be suitable for all audiences, particularly children and young adults.

The author and publisher acknowledge the sensitive nature of these topics and have

Shanaya Stephens

made every effort to handle them with respect and care. However, we recognize that reading about these themes can be distressing and potentially triggering.

If you are experiencing distress or need support, please reach out to a trusted adult, mental health professional, or call a helpline such as the National Suicide Prevention Lifeline (1-800-273-TALK (8255) in the US) or a local crisis centre.

Remember, your well-being and safety are important. Please prioritize them when reading this book.

Author's note

When I started writing these stories, I had no idea what I was doing with them. Within the course of twenty-four hours, I squeezed my heart out to give you this… 'Strangers on the Internet'.

The fact that it was written literally within a day, should suffice to say that this isn't monumental writing. This is one of my most raw, served hot, straight from the heart works.

Now, it's all yours. Do what you will with it.

Love,
Shanaya Stephens

1. Disclaimer 4
2. Author's note 6
3. Krist, or the one with a catalyst 10
4. Dan, or the one who wanted to escape his skin 16
5. Nika, or the one who got away 29
6. Archi, or the predatory butthole ... 40
7. Kamaal, or the one who fulfilled the prophecy 54
8. Kasper, or the father who had failed 60
9. Molly, or the one who couldn't leave 67
10. Acknowledgments 79
11. About the author 80
12. About the book 82
13. Other Titles By the Author 83

Strangers On the Internet

"We all consume lies when our heart is hungry."

Shanaya Stephens

Krist, or the one with a catalyst

It was a battle of wits on a Saturday night. To know what to do when one figures out, they might never be truly loved by another being; especially their parents. With legs crossed, lying on her generic bed; Krist didn't bother patting her aching thigh. She could feel the pulse of her calf, as snoot collected on the corner of her eye.

A blurry lining of mucous plastered her pupil, through which she could perfectly well see the bright glow of the pink camera icon. All that she knew about a pretty, and ideal world came from that part of the internet. On her best days, Krist would smile and comment on most of what people had to say about their lives, or other people's lives for that matter. Not once did she feel she was prying in because let's face it, why would people even post on the internet if they didn't want to hear a scandalous thing or two?

Shanaya Stephens

Krist had hoped this early bout of emotional dump would end by the night. But sadly, it had just begun to hit her. It was the third day of her period. For anyone who had said 'third's a charm', had probably never thought it through. In all its capacity, her uterus had waged a war against her sniffing being.

It was quite a sight then - a depraved, twenty-year-old, curled up on a bed that she shared with her other sister at her parents' place. None of these parents who had quite known what to do with both of them, had thought it best to shove them in the corner room like most people who have a farm do with their squeaky chickens. Sadly, for Krist, she would never be able to lure them into loving her with her eggs. If anything, the fact that she could in fact have eggs made her more of a liability.

"So, what do you want to do next?" Someone has asked Krist when they found out she was graduating. If she could be honest about it, she would go with something like - get an ice-cream, or maybe, die. Krist took the world one day at a time, so this paramount struggle of having it come all at once to her was largely unwelcomed.

Strangers On the Internet

The world had to suck, there was no other way she could be so overwhelmed because of it. To avoid suspicion that she was borderline suicidal Krist would say, "I think it looks a little cool to have something to do with biology," and nod her head in the way people do when they want to convince someone that they understand, but in all honesty, they just want to go home and sleep.

Sadly, sleep was something that came to Krist easy. It was sad because then she had little or no time with her grief. She would try to think about changing things, but not enough to lose sleep over them. Then she would have the most vivacious dreams. In one of those, her favourite stand-up comedian would slyly lay her down on the living room couch and make love to her. In her dreams there was no reason, just love. The guy, although she knew pretty well which one it ought to be, always remained faceless. Every next day, Krist had to wake up from that dream. The reality was not so full of love. It sucked.

Krist lied on her back, when she was halfway through a comment. She wasn't happy at all. This comment was not supposed to be a happy one, either. It was a condescending one. On a rate of one to ten, it was eleven when it came to being mean. She was doing it purposefully. Her bad day deserved to have extended to all those who were too happy for the world. Krist wasn't going to go to bed alone with those thoughts, in her skinny pink vest and borrowed shorts. Even if she could go to bed with it, she had clearly chosen not to. Not everything in her life was about sacrifices anyway. She did her part in making herself seem a lot more human when she was on the internet.

"Cut some fat, balloon," she had hit enter. It wasn't even supposed to be a fat shaming comment. The girl in the picture seemed too skinny to ever be moderately fat. Someone called P*eony_Pats. It was such a phony name!* To Krist it seemed the best thing to do since, one, skinny people are not thick skinned so they get offended easily, *duh*. Two, it was nice to make people insecure when her whole world was falling apart. Then, it made two of them so she didn't have to do it alone!

The deed was done. A fresh breath of air entered her, and ended with a shallow sniff.

Strangers On the Internet

She was about to sneeze, but then comments popped on her phone. Of course, she wasn't dumb enough to comment on a rookie influencer's post. She had gone for the most famous one. People flooded the replies with slurs, and words you can barely say at the Church. Her sad eyes twinkled. For this misery that she had self-induced, she was the one in control. It would take one 'delete', and all the people would be left wondering what just happened.

People on the internet seemed to have no life of their own. Krist seemed to have understood that bit herself well. Part of it was because Krist didn't quite have one herself. She was friendless in the most amiable way.

When she had graduated high school, COVID had swept the world back into their homes. Krist's mom best believed that her girls be kept in isolation from the rest of the world. For as long, forever. It seemed to have worked in nobody's favour. Now Krist hated going outside, and her mom hated Krist. There was not much to say about her dad either. If not for him, Krist would have not lost her sense of coherence.

Shanaya Stephens

Now, she was sloppy and slow. Getting hit by a man does that to you. Especially if that man is your father. Krist now, thought that it was best to do what was asked of her. To get money. But she didn't know the how, or the why of it. So here she was, on the internet.

Dan, or the one who wanted to escape his skin

Dan had just poured in five new shots of Mojito. That is, if one can call them shots. Saturday was the worst day to wait tables at a bar. It was fucking Giaret's! Every bartender's dark, wet dream. And now, he had to shake, ice, slide and smile for an eternity. He wanted to leave a long while ago. Unlike those whose dream job was infact, to be a bar tender, Dan was here because he had nowhere else to be.

He had put on the cheap Giaret's uniform that came in only shades of black. A stupid apron sat on his lanky body, and he tried not to remind himself about his dues. A big ass G was embossed in the seams of his apron, with a fancy text in cursive that read: 'This or nothing".

As if...This was the last place he wanted to be. If it wasn't the money, he would pack

Shanaya Stephens

his bags and leave the States. Being there did things to him. It made him overtly aware of the fact that he was missing life.

Everyday was like clockwork. There was no means to escape the routine. Wake up, shit, clean, work, and try hard to not die. It was nothing less than clinical. He lived two blocks from the bar. He never wanted to start here in the first place. Some waitress had fucked the boss, and was fired because she was humping another guy at work. They wanted someone who would suck up to the boss again. He just happened to be the fit candidate. He was lone, desperate, broke and essentially, an immigrant.

This was the worst thing that had happened to him. He hated this country, not because it was nothing like his own, but because it could never be. And then there was the genetics. His face wasn't something that sat on his neck awkwardly. But he was too worried about being judged. His eyes. His eyes gave him away. And then there were the eyes of those who would stare longer than they wanted to. Especially those women who came after eleven. There were weak moments where he wanted to crawl out of his skin to avoid an awkward conversation.

There was this sly smugness about them. These women were so sure of themselves that even if they had one, runny mascara lined cheek, they could get a man to take themselves home. Dan could only imagine what it would mean to be like that. He had never dated in whatever teen years he had in his life. He wasn't too old now, but he was significantly older. Starting young does that to you.

Dan, when asked what he wanted from his life, would always say something abstract. Like peace, or freedom. He had started dreaming in the lands that were smaller than his dreams. He was somewhat of an artist like that. When he left home, he wanted to do epic shit. What he didn't know that it took Van Gogh, a life time, and only death made him famous. He had forgotten that faraway lands are kinder to none, and that good things will always take time. He realised he didn't have much of it... Time, or life, for that matter.

Where he came from, Dan was taught that there was nothing so unsure about a man's existence than the size of his dick. It had got to him early in his life. His awareness about his not so manly body, had made him so sour he would not even try to make an effort. Crippling anxiety, bawling hours in the bathroom, and a life with no dates between the sheets had made him certain. His life was a poor excuse for stalling death. He was no man. He was a nobody.

The bar usually opened after six, but he would show up an hour before. He would willingly take on the cleaning duties. When he was not running a rag on the counter, he swiped through the stash of Us Weekly. Not for the gossip. For whatever section had something on "how to be man". Sometimes, he would sneak in a camera at the back of the men's stall. At first, he was appalled by the fact that he was filming pissing men, who for the record didn't wash their hands after. But then, he had a greater sense of pity for himself than the urge to respect the privacy of a bunch of unhygienic men.

He watched the recordings after his shift was done. Aware that it might have caught something, he didn't dare touch the camera again, after the fifth day. For some reason, the camera remained intact. Nobody knew.

Dan would compare sizes every night when his little hell of a shift came to an end. His phone would floppy over his bed, and he would set his member free. He would first scale it up, and then look at it for long. When it first started, he hoped for an epiphany. He needed an epiphany. Guilt used to show up every now and then. He would have loved to stop then, but now... Not so often.

Dan had a singular perspective in his life now, which birthed a rather shallow motive for him. To be so beautiful that no one can question his authority. But he was also told that men are not beautiful. They can never be beautiful, in fact. They were supposed to be handsome. What handsome people do is, carry a big D size. They have hairy chests, and crested abs. They do not talk politely. They seldom smile. They are mysterious. They like to fuck girls every weekend. Dan wasn't sure if he liked any of those things at all. There was no such thing as a handsome, immigrant bartender anyway. It's always that Chinese boy who cannot speak good English for him.

Yet, Dan thought it was easy to be polite, to be kind, to not fuck girls, and to not have abs. But that only meant that he cannot be handsome, ever. It was too late to worry over things like that now. His shift had begun an hour ago. Dan let out a sigh, and handed the girls their drinks. His face had started to resemble the saggy state of his balls. The idea was revolting.

Another hour clocked in. A man walked in, and Dan forced his smile again. It was pathetic at first. Then, it slowly, smoothly curled around the edges. It wasn't forced now. His eyes gleamed with something hopeful. The man was young, and he didn't slap his butt yet. Knowing that he might not be one of those jerks helped. It was the sort of admiration that came from meeting someone who had everything you ever wanted. The man certainly looked like he didn't smile, had a bad boy between his pants, and loved to smooch and tongue girls. He wore cool tones. Dan gave him a once over, before the guy offered a 'Hi!'.

Dan offered the pleasantries. "What would you have?" The accent hadn't faded. He hadn't become any more American than he was a minute ago.

Strangers On the Internet

One shot of whisky and some obscene liquor. On Rocks. It was a relatively simple order. Basic.

"Coming, right up."

He nodded, and was back to the bottles. He had poured him a nice glass, slide it over, and hoped for a smile. It never came. He ogled at the guy, as he gulped it all down at once. His eyebrows shot up at Dan.

"What time do you get off work?" The man asked, and Dan looked at him confused. Was something wrong? He didn't say much. Then a weak 'two in the morning', slipped out of his tongue.

"I'll see you then," the guy offered, and slipped off to one of those booths in the back.

Dan thought nothing of it. He had more drinks to make. The man however couldn't keep his eyes off the bar. He hadn't batted an eye to all the other girls at the bar. Some of them had flashed him in a vain attempt to catch his eye.

Shanaya Stephens

He kept ordering random things. The last time Dan checked; it was peanuts. Two hit the clock hard, and Dan was ready to go about his business. He would probably watch some more guys on the tape, or worse, try to catch some sleep.

"Dan?" To his amusement, the guy from the bar hadn't left yet.

"What do you want now?" It was the first time Dan had actually spoken to someone in a week. Actually spoken, and not felt anything uncanny about it.

"I was wondering if you'd like to come home with me," the man offered, and Dan scrunched his face in disgust. "What are you?" Dan asked, and he curled his fingers around Dan's wrist.

"You smiled at me. You looked like you were sad. I can make you some happy," the guy chuckled, and Dan shook his head in disdain.

No, he couldn't possibly hope for things like that from a man. What does he possibly know about making him happy?

"I would rather get going," Dan dismissed him.

"Why don't you understand?" He had pulled him too close now. Their faces were inches away.

"If you don't like it, all you have to do is to ask me to stop. It'll be worth your time. *Worth our time,*" the man proposed, before he dragged him back to the restroom at the back of the bar.

Dan could have screamed, or asked for help. But that won't be very manly of him. This was the first time something like this had happened. He had quite not known what it felt like to be wanted. The man made him feel wanted. For better, or worse, he needed to know if he could be pulled out from his self-loathing by the virtue of being desired.

He followed the big, bulky guy to the back of the stall. Dan knew there was a camera somewhere there. He pushed Dan against the wall, as his eyes searched for the camera.

"I am really into you," the guy said, and Dan couldn't help but feel the bulge between his pants. Was this it? His life long obsession with dicks had made him crave it so much that he was sporting a hard on when a man, that huge, wanted to do things to him? His mother would have been so disappointed. A tear trickled down his cheek.

"I am sorry. I do not understand. I am not..." Dan staggered, but the man's hands had already slid down his butt. He had just removed enough clothes to get access. Dan's body wasn't anything sort of remarkable. It was just alright, if not *fine*.

"What are you doing?" Dan didn't stop him yet. He was just surprised that a man would make him feel things like that. His head touched the wall, as he sat on the can. His eyes were dreamy, and rolled back in his head. He could feel his warm mouth around him. It wasn't comfortable, but it didn't make him want to run away. At least, not yet.

His climax built up, against his gut. He was so close to finding his release. And then... His thoughts spiralled back to the size of his dick. The slickness that wrapped around the punny thing. Disgusting. All he could think of was the dicks that had plastered onto the camera. The camera who was watching the strange, big man undone his jeans and the big O of his mouth as he took Dan in, the way Dan's body jerked, and how the two of them sweated and moaned. It made Dan sick. The idea of him ruining the beautiful mouth of the man that knelt before him.

When the man was done, Dan couldn't recognise himself. Perhaps, he was different now. Maybe he was different before. He felt worse than he did before.

"You are so good," the man said before he unbuckled his own pants. He yanked Dan up by brute force. His jaw hurt, as he forced his mouth open. The man wasn't as big as he thought. He was uncircumcised. His tip was too big for Dan to even try to wrap his tongue around it. The man wasn't considerate enough to ask Dan. Dan didn't have the space to ask questions, or offer his counsel. His dick stuffed in Dan's face, and he couldn't wait for it to come to an end.

The man said something along the lines of 'please', 'sorry', and 'thank you'. Dan didn't pay attention. He was waiting for him to leave. Even if it was a bit awkward, and that it was on a tape that he would be watching later that night. His chest fell deeply, as the man zipped himself up and left. He realised his face was wet, and his mouth was dripping with drool, and semen.

He reached for the tissue, and tore pieces of it. He wiped the corners of his mouth. The taste still lingered on his tongue. He couldn't take it. He stuffed wads of tissue into his mouth. The papery taste was dry against his tongue. He shoved them all the way to his throat. The man hadn't been there, but he didn't want to take chances. His face was soaked, as he choked on the paper.

His body went limp. His face had turned red. He wanted to be cleaner. Remove any trace of the man on his skin. Dan reached for the camera. Crushed it with the blow of his palm. More tears ran down his face. He realised that his mom would be disappointed in him, but he wasn't. A notification buzzed in his pocket. He reached for his phone. He no longer wanted to be beautiful. He didn't want to be there. He didn't want to be. He didn't.

Strangers On the Internet

The screen lit up. His tears stilled into drops over it. The splitting light casted a spectrum. How ironic!

It was a random picture now, but the comments were blowing up. The stupid app. The stupid, stupid app. Those girls. The beautiful girls. Everything he never was, or would be. And there they were...One of those hot divas on the app... He stared at the screen in a dazed, in the aftermath of his post climax blues. He wanted to do something, anything.

He didn't remember the relevance of it all, but all he did was type. "Maybe you should get sucked at the back of a stall", hit enter and then slip it back into his pocket. Dan no longer had to worry about his dick. He had bigger problems now. He hated everything in the world, and all that came with it.

Shanaya Stephens

Nika, or the one who got away

Giving birth is like shitting. It gets stuck, and it hurts to get it out. Turns out that you really shit yourself when you give birth. Nika's experience was no less wonderful. She watched her nurse stick her hand in places she would not normally let a woman touch. The doctor had told her something about the baby a second ago, but she couldn't seem to get it. Or, keep track of things for that matter.

The pain was crushing. Her uterus felt like it was going to split in half. This wasn't her first time. But nothing prepares you for this. This obscene amount of pain that churns out a ball of life out of you. And then years spent to look after this new being. Children… If it weren't for the raging hormones, she wouldn't have inflicted this on herself.

She was only forty-two, after all. She had the virtue of ageing slow, and her body could put those in their twenties to shame. But right now, she looked old. Strands of black hair stuck to her forehead. Her cheeks had put up fat, and she was a big woman now. Pregnancy cravings were showing up in all her curves, and she no longer liked it. She took shallow breaths, as the contractions rolled in. Her face had turned red.

"God, the fuck is this baby going to get out," she screamed, hoarsely.

The nurses minded their own business. Shit always went down at the labour's room. They had asked her 'family' to be prepared for what was to come. It seemed to have worked well in nobody's favour. Her cervix externa had torn open. They didn't want to use the forceps.

"Darling, can you please keep your voice down. It's annoying the nurses!" He had urged her. She had looked him in the eye, and told him to "fuck off". He might have taken it to heart. The baby was coming down.

That was ten minutes ago. Nika's husband had passed out on the floor. His big, bald head has developed a crack. Blood had oozed out of it. When the baby's head popped out of her vagina, he just couldn't look at it anymore. Years of fantasy that he had brewed for him and his wife, was coming to an end. Part of the reason why he couldn't take it was because now, sex wouldn't be the same. She wouldn't be as tight. "Fuck, that's my baby," he wailed, and that was the last of him for the hour.

The nurses cursed, and had shifted him to a suitable place. He was more nuisance than Nika herself. But that's just how it was with men. They moved him close by. A room where he was treated for his injury, but not for his misogyny. If he could now help it, he would have just adopted a kid from one of those flyers they handed out at signals. But it was too late to reconsider. Nika wouldn't be as tight anymore when he would enter her. Yes, the thought was horrifying. He had only married her so that he could fuck her seven days, a week for the rest of his life. That was rather presumptuous of him, for he, as Nika would put it, "Had the shorter end of the stick. Could barely do it for ten minutes." But that also meant they would save plenty of time.

They had met each other four years ago, at his office party. He had a wife then. She was fucking her boss. They exchanged smiles, numbers, and then sneaked into the little store room at the bar. They banged each other, and he made her come twice. The storeroom smelled like Lysol and white-man semen. Nika knew she couldn't do better. It was a sealed deal. They had to fuck more.

Nika no longer believed in love when she met him. "That was white-people shit," she said. And, he was whiter than any guy she had the privilege to fuck. She knew it wasn't really true. Because, for one, where she came from, she did find herself a really white dude. He was just Asian. They fucked good, and long. He was nothing like her husband. Which is why, he left. And here she was.

Their affair, for everyone's good lasted for a week. Later, his wife would find out and they would divorce. Her boss would fire her for the fear of STIs. Nika was homeless then. Her one-night stand, for the weeks to come, was remotely wifeless. It seemed like a perfect match. So, they hastily married at a Church. He didn't bother getting her a real wedding dress. She filed the paperwork. There, after years of fucking around she had finally found the secret to a happy life. Fucking American citizenship.

Ten years ago, Nika, flew halfway across the world from Vietnam to Sussex. She just wanted a life beyond her mother's. Her dad had high hopes for her. She failed to be any of those things that they wanted her to be. She wanted a family that could provide for her. The lives they lived were too half, and she wasn't born to be poor. So, she ran away from home with her then boyfriend. He seemed like a nice guy, but he was a really bad idea. Nika, it turns out, had miscarried his baby before she landed a job as a waitress at Giaret's. It had been years. Lines had blurred, and he was nothing but a bad memory.

That was all in the past. Now the baby was delivered. It was a boy, and he looked nothing like Nika. Her legs were still widely spread, and she worried about her husband. What if he refuses to fuck her? Not that she wanted him to. Given that it had led to this waking nightmare.

Nika looked at the baby in the cradle. It had cried itself pink, and the nurses did everything in their power to make him shut up. But that's the thing about babies. They cannot be silenced into omission by the world's will. Nika then had to take him and rock him to sleep. They offered to look after him for a bit, while the nurses cleaned her. Her husband was still passed out. She mumbled a silent prayer. Perhaps, she hadn't been all American yet.

Nika watched the boy sleep. It almost seemed lifeless at first. On a closer look, Nika would see a rise, and fall of chest under the cloth that wrapped the baby. For a moment, he seemed so beautiful. He seemed perfect. Then the impending pain crawled to her. Her back was hurting, her perineum was obliterated, and her vagina felt abused. This was bad.

"We would give you a minute to yourself," the nurses had told her when they scraped off the last bit of poop and blood from her butt. They wanted to feel sorry for her, but it wasn't a new thing in the labour room. It happened every day. Nika was not the worst they had seen. Nika wouldn't be the last they would ever see. For that matter, she didn't really make a difference.

Nika asked for pills. Something for pain, soon after. Her husband had still not found himself conscious. Nobody commented on how it could all be a staged act. Not even the nurses who knew it was impossible to pass out, and not wake up six hours after. They collectively decided to not talk about it. "The husband was sleeping like an ass," they established. Nods went around. The doctor came, and checked the baby. He gave them a green signal to go back home. Nika had still not recovered. She lazily asked, "Can't we stay here a day more?"

"I am afraid not. Your insurance barely covers it," the doctor said, and Nika nodded. Nika wanted to use the washroom. She wanted to pee. She wasn't even sure if she could use her pee hole. There was only one way to find out. She slowly walked to the washroom. The door gave up easily. She sat on the can, with the big diaper on. It was for the blood. She was losing a lot of blood.

It had been years, and she had not once looked back to reminisce. She had been, and out of love. She went to great lengths not to. Her husband, was someone she had chosen not to fall in love with. She fucked him so passionately; he would never know the difference. But now, things would change. Perhaps, he would realize how lacklustre it was. Men, ah men. She best thought them like a disease. They made her so vulnerable, and so uncomfortable in her own skin when they owned her. When she tried to heal herself of it, she would feel guilty. It's just what they do. These men. These vile men. Thankfully, her husband was only half a man. It made him somewhat tolerable. To know he didn't fully possess her made her feel free. It was a gamble, but she had done it well. A life of pleasure, for the lack of love.

Nika didn't pee. Instead, she cried. She bawled out in the washroom, relieved to an extent that nobody heard her. She wanted to go back home. Not really. He wouldn't take care of her if she does. She couldn't stay either. But now, she was a baby mother. She had no idea how to raise a fucking child. Her husband was a lost cause. Maybe she would screw herself up again. Maybe she will forge a way out. There was no telling. She was too old to be so brave, but then she was a mother now. Doesn't motherhood make the silliest of them into such brave beings? At least on the internet. The internet. Perhaps, that's what she needed.

Shanaya Stephens

It was quite strange, at first. Nika wasn't allowed a phone in the hospital. So, she realised she couldn't really cry in the washroom and hope for things to get better. She needed to be on the app. She still didn't pee.

She had asked her nurse for her phone. They told her she didn't infact come with her phone to the hospital. Nika looked at the nurse questioningly. Her husband in the meantime, was up and ready to take the baby with him. He had been too joyous for the occasion. "Perhaps, it was the baby, or his ardent love for her," the nurses exchanged glances.

"Baby, I need your phone," Nika said, and she got it. Her husband watched the baby, and didn't ask her much. He just nodded, and held the baby in his arms. In the fifty years of his life, he hadn't been much of an honest man. With Nika, he didn't want to start a family. He wasn't ready to be a father, and he knew it. When she was six months in, he had called his ex-wife and spent the night in her bed. He had a feeling Nika knew about it. None of them had brought it up. He never had kids from the other marriage, but now...This was different. The baby had his eyes, and he just cannot overlook it. Maybe he will learn to love the boy. Maybe he would go back to his ex. There was no telling. He didn't like to pretend about caring, as such. But this boy...This boy with bright blue eyes was his. He would learn to hold onto that. The baby had calmed down since he had scooped him in his arms. To Nika, he couldn't yet bear to say much. There was no 'how are you feeling', 'do you need something', or a half willed 'I love you'.

The follower count had grown on the App, ever since her husband posted about it. That was a good sign. She had gone through a whole nine months, doing weird trends to catch the algorithm. Nika was on and about all things on the Internet, till they earned the blue tick. She hadn't quite learned to let go of that. This baby was going to make her famous, and by some miracle, instil love back in her life. She didn't want to cry. This was the life she worked for. Maybe not all of it, but surely some of it. She waved at the camera, and turned it to her husband. He was still holding onto the baby. "We are a family of three now!" All exhaustion that had painted her face was well masked with a smile that didn't touch her eyes.

Nika asked the nurse to click a picture of the three of them. Nika looked ugly in the picture. Her face was without makeup, and she looked her age. Forty-two, and a mother. "Nothing that cannot be fixed by a filter," she thought. She slapped one on it, and posted it within the next few seconds.

The phone slid back to her husband's pockets. A ringing beep hummed its tune there. He read the comments to her. Nika smiled for the first time in forty-eight hours. "People think we have a beautiful boy!" Nika said, and her husband nodded. Maybe, there was hope.

Archi, or the predatory butthole

Archi decided it was best done now. This whole new app for social media thing... He had big plans for this one. His eyes squinted, as he settled on a username. It should feel real, not cliche, and most of all; not give him away. He settled with the one that seemed normal to most others at the time. @thejokerpoet. It didn't seem to have much to it. It wasn't very tacky, but it couldn't be dismissed for a pretentious bot either.

If he had learnt anything about the internet, it was that people always seemed to have ungodly kindness for pity stories. He had tried his hand at other platforms before, and the results were spectacular. But not the app. Especially, not the app. He couldn't quite decide what had made him hold back but now he was here. Things had changed.

He had just got a new girlfriend. The last seven of his were such a bad influence on him, he knew their moods by the back of his hand. They had all called him some names and left, for good or worse. He often pictured his heart broken into seven, fat pieces. Each being fed on by a crow, as blood oozed out of his being. It helped to think of things in a manner that made him more of a victim, and less of a perpetrator. He had mastered the art by now. Start smooth, lure them in, act wounded, and then... He sat on the precipice of being a full-fledged, serial dater. Multi-dater? Digital fuckboy? No, that sounded bad. Perhaps, he would go with Loverboy. That seemed less dubious, indeed.

The screen flashed bright before him. He had already custom made a bunch of posts from poetry he had quietly plagiarised from his ex-partners. They were all custom edited on Canva, and bore a meek watermark of his username to claim it as his. These were just to get him started. He would borrow some cheesy words from internet later. Anything would do for now, he thought.

He shuffled the posts. It was hard to pick one. Which one could possibly be the subtlest of them? It should make him seem heartbroken enough, but not be a trauma dump. His options seemed limited, now that he had a content preference.

The girls he had dated were younger than him. He would tell them he was seventeen, and handsomely young. Which was like, the other lies of his, easily bought. He knew how to be an incriminating idiot, and worked well to stay in the character. His life, if nothing was an act of deception. How he had started this rampage of collecting hearts online was a mystery to himself too!

Perhaps it was his father. His father was an astute man who had little time for his family. His mother couldn't be bothered with his nonsense. Between his parents, who were working nine to five, and him and his little sister; he wasn't even a choice. Things had gotten a lot worse after they realised that he was a terrible influence on the young one. He wanted to be loved out of need.

Shit hadn't gone down yet. Like all good stories, his also starts with the power of internet (in its full glory, I am afraid). He had thought it was the perfect day to do the deed. He had brought in all things he deemed necessary. A pack of tissues, a pillow, and a bottle of water. His laptop sat lazily against the desk with a black screen that read 'Incognito'.

It started off really well. He had heard his friends doing it often, when they found themselves alone. He coiled his fingers around the shaft. They pumped him good, and well. His high caught onto him. But, this wasn't supposed to be a story with a happy ending. Fate had big plans for him, and his dick.

His sister, had accidentally walked in on him wanking to a model on his computer. She couldn't quite know what that was about. Her face had dropped, and there was nothing but blatant horror with which she looked at him. She went on to tell her mom, and her mom to her dad. He knew then, and there that he was long gone. He would never be seen the same way. All his longing, and sadness had culminated into something worse. There was no way he would walk through this life alone. All good ideas are birthed from need. Here was his... To have people at his beck and call. No amount of masturbating would fill that void. Turns out he needed something to believe in too.

Strangers On the Internet

He was twenty-five now. He had moved out to live with his uncle. His uncle had moved out to live with his wife. He decided it was best to live alone for his newly found ventures then. He wanted to be loved. By this time, he had firmly believed it can only be done so well by a woman. If there was anything that a woman cannot get rid of, it was her kindness. And young girls were half the woman, which made them over brimming with more hormones and just the perfect amount of kindness.

Some nights, he would sit with his knees to his chest and question life, and love. Not everything had to be bad about him. He believed there was nothing wrong to want to be loved. Humans were born with the innate need to be loved. It wasn't until his sister had cut ties with him that he realized that, maybe not everyone was capable of loving him. It made him sad. Then one fine evening he met her.

He was lying on the diwan with a notification about assignments. His best part of the day had ended at the practice nets. There was no subtlety about the fact that life was giving him shit.

Shanaya Stephens

College gets to most of us when we are not looking. He, in particular, wasn't good with the propriety of a stellar student. There must be something that could make the ends meet, he thought. He was quick to text someone who knew what to do. She was a girl, yes. And out of whatever kindness she had in her heart, she agreed to help. He only had to lie about his mother being too sick.

Don't worry. I can understand. It's not easy for everyone. She had written to him. He just pinged her with a nonchalant 'true that', with his fingers dwindling in the packet of Cheetos. Just like that, things were done. A heavy weight lifted off his shoulder.

Finally, a good post.

The life we live,
Takes from us all
But love
And love is what
Makes life
Suffice.

@jokerpoet.

He had posted the one his new girlfriend had wrote to him. The lines were hardly poetry. But people loved exaggerating shit on the internet. Everyone who commented on these posts had a potential to be a middle grade English teacher. These people would squeeze inferences out of shit. That by itself was a downside to the internet. People thought too much. People had too much free time. That was more than half of the demography on the new app! But it would work well for him, anyways. Relieved he had set his base; he texted his new girlfriend.

She hadn't replied yet. A worrying wrinkle settled on his forehead. It was so not nice of her to not reply to him on time. He had big plans for her. He wanted her to send him pictures. He needed those pictures for his lone time. It helped a lot to have pictures.

He had started this practice after his third girlfriend. It helped him plan the stakes. With all due respect, time was of essence. He didn't want to be there for the ugly ducklings. People always want what they cannot have, and he was in no possession of beauty. Of course, he lacked integrity, self-esteem, empathy, and values; but they didn't interfere with his core need to be loved. And this girl, this new girlfriend, if for the lack of a better word was 'annoying'.

Shanaya Stephens

When they started dating online, he would send her kiss GIFs, and she would blush, or act naively. After a few days, she started to send him romantic quotes. She said something about waiting till marriage. God knows who she was saving her hymen for. He didn't really know about hymen until his sixth girlfriend. No, they did not fuck. But she fucked his friend.

Time flew by, and he waited for the pictures. The pictures didn't come. The day had passed. He knew he could just call her, but he didn't want to grow attached. It made him uncomfortable to ever develop feelings for one of those many girls. Feelings were like throwing stones at a hornet's nest. Nobody voluntarily did it. It was an honest mistake. If he ever came close, he would have them blocked, or talk shit about their family. It always worked.

Two days had passed away. She hadn't texted him back. He was going berserk, little by little. This wasn't a part of the plan. Then, someone did text him. It was a new girl on the app. Some bigshot influencer. God, she was hot.

Strangers On the Internet

He thought she was into him. A solitary heart rested in his comment section. That was it. Even when he thought he was different from them, he wasn't really different from them. At the end of the day, he was just a dick. Dicks don't think. They fuck. The text was even more suggestive. She wrote a 'Hiii'. One must be nothing less of a stupid to think she wasn't thinking about him all day, all long, waiting for his reply.

He was convinced he was man of the minute. So, in the confidence of his bedroom he texted her. They talked for a long while that night. Most of it was a lie, often two sided.

Peony_Pats:Do you like The Smiths?

Ofc. I like all of them.
He only knew two of them. The goldsmith, and the blacksmith.

Peony_Pats:Do you have any hobbies?

Oh yes, cricket.
He had only ever played with the children down the block.

Shanaya Stephens

Peony_Pats:Do you have any dreams?

I want to be an aeronautical engineer. I love the sky.
He didn't graduate high school. He worked at Domino's briefly before going to online classes. He was failing this semester too.

Peony_Pats:You sound like an adventurous guy! Are you dom or sub?
Ofc, Dom!
He worked at Dominos! Ta da! Solidarity.

Peony_Pats:Damn, Daddy!
Not your daddy, because I am young. But you can call me love.
What's wrong with this *gore log*?

By this time, his annoyance with his new girlfriend was almost forgotten. A guy like him could have any other girl. She wasn't that special. That's what the new girl had told him, and he believed it wholeheartedly.

Three days passed, and the girl hadn't texted him yet. She, and her pictures were both forgotten. Archi had started to forget what she looked like. He no longer waited for her at night. He had good company, despite her absence.

Strangers On the Internet

The new girl had managed to charm him. They talked over voice call on the fourth day. She sounded vaguely familiar, but he couldn't quite put his finger on it. She was an influencer. He probably saw her on reels. She sounded lovely. He was tempted to ask her for pictures. He knew she would have offered within a passage of time. But then, the fifth day had come and nothing happened. She hadn't even returned his hugs. She was just too nice to him. It made him insufferable. *Could they please just skip to the sexting?*

On the sixth day, he faintly remembered he had a girlfriend. He had almost started to miss her. At least, she looked like a good lay. But he couldn't quite remember her face, now. He was mildly disappointed. All this time, he was used to people acting the way he wanted them to. And the new girl wasn't helping his dick much.

He rang her up, on the seventh day. There was no point in second guessing now. Someone had already picked up the call. The voice didn't seem girly in particular, and now he was tense.

Shanaya Stephens

"Hello, am I talking to..."

Before he could speak more, the man on the other end said solemnly. "I am her father. If you know what's better for you, you would stay away from her. I will turn you in, to the police if you don't."

All colours faded from his face, as he sat there dumb. Was that girl too dense? Who the fuck tells their parents about the guy they are dating? Especially online! God, this was for the better. He didn't want to end up in jail. He wasn't really seventeen, either. He would fuck up bad, if he did end up in jail. The call ended. He understood what to do.

The following evening, his phone buzzed again. He typed out ingeniously.

I think I love you, Peony. But can you keep a secret?

She hadn't replied for an hour.

Peony_Pats:hi
archi
I was just taking a shower.
OMG, really?

Strangers On the Internet

Yes! Would you like to go out with me?

Peony_Pats:Typing...
I would

Peony_Pats:Typing...
But

Peony_Pats:Typing...
I
Have
One
Condition.

Peony_Pats:Typing...
Can I see what you look like down there?

Was this God's grace? He wondered. But what did she mean by down there?

Tell me what you want babe. Something from your book page? I can give it to you. You can call me Zade.
These lines were plagiarised from a reel on the App itself.

Peony_Pats:I want to see what your dick looks like, darling.

Shanaya Stephens

The app had served his purpose. He now had a new girlfriend!

Strangers On the Internet

Kamaal, or the one who fulfilled the prophecy

Kamaal had just killed his brother. The trails of red blood had marked his living room. Outside, the wedding band was playing a rigged version of 'Video Killed the Radio Star'. He wasn't sure what to do with the body. *Maano na mere yaar*...He just sat there, thinking long enough for the stench to fill the room. *Oh aa oh aa*...He wanted to slap his face again, and again. He should have done that before stabbing him. But this was also alright. He can no longer bother his waifu. *Tumse hai tumse pyaar-*

Kamaal and his brother, had a feud. It wasn't for the sake of inheritance unlike most other brothers, but for a woman. This woman, they hadn't met her yet. But God, she was beautiful.

They had stumbled upon her profile on the app. It was a beautiful picture. She was sporting a linen shirt. It was white, and sat softly against her curves. She was Norwegian, they presumed (it was written in her profile). Her front curved into two juicy balls, and she only wore cool tones. Kamaal loved cool tones on women. He was tired of watching women in black abayas, and burkhas anyway. He absolutely adored the way she had carried herself in the videos.

She had ocean blue eyes, and they had a mysterious edge to them. Surely, he won't find anyone like that in the whole of Peshawar. Kamaal, here, was a learned man. He excelled in everything, but romance. It seemed like the perfect opportunity to start. He wanted to whisk her away from the seams of the world, the moment he had laid eyes on her. But his brother was always in the way. He had started to hate him because of it.

She is just a model, his brother would say. *Why would she possibly fall for someone like you?* He would question Kamaal. Kamaal would want to hit him hard on the head, right then. But the grimacing faces of his Abba and Ammi would make him stop. It slowly started to get out of hand.

One day, Kamaal had come home to find his brother doing the dishes. He jested about him being wife less. Kamaal's brother was way too old to not be married. Where he came from, marriage was an important aspect of a man's identity. Kamaal knew that he had to marry the most beautiful woman of them all, or he would forever be mocked.

Unlike Kamaal, his brother would stay far from marital affairs. This brother of his, was an oddball in the world of racing rats. He was some sort of mystic. Shutting himself in the corner of his room, he would weave poetry with ink, and hide them between pages of some book. Mir Taqi Mir, Faiz, and Faraz would shake their heads at him. Kamaal's brother was somewhat of a romantic. But he believed love couldn't be found on the app. It was this profound revelation that had driven Kamaal to the edge of insanity.

Kamaal's mother found it disheartening to have two different sons, lost in their own worlds. Both of them had refused to marry in the neighbourhood for very different reasons. She could no longer go to social events without being looked down upon. They had started asking her if her sons had all their manly parts, or were they perhaps born with defects? At this, Kamaal's mother would quote what Kamaal had so ingeniously asked her to, "My youngest one, Kamaal, has already gotten a lady in his life. She is in Norway, and she is very beautiful." To this the woman would gasp, and remove their shawls. This went on for quite a few weeks until one fine day, one of them asked him, "Does this daughter-in-law of yours know she is your daughter in law? What does she even do? How have we not seen her yet?" To this, Kamaal's mother had no answer. She would swallow her pride, and smile as if that was all it would take to stop the rumours from spreading.

Like all bad things that occur at social events, this one led to the downfall of a seemingly happy family. Kamaal's mother came home that evening with tears in her eyes. She blamed, and cajoled her cruel sons and their poor conduct. She had hated the fact that she was becoming the butt of every joke in the neighbourhood. None of her sons possibly reacted to any of these things, until she said..."This Norwegian Bahu... I want you to bring her home!"

The house went eerily silent. Nobody knew what was to be done. Kamaal's Abbu retired to his bed. He was too old to deal with undisciplined boys. Kamaal's brother was the first to speak, "Mom, he cannot marry her. She doesn't even know him. And she couldn't possibly marry him even if he convinced her!" He then mocked with a snorting laughter. For Kamaal, it was a little too much.

"What do you mean?" Kamaal asked, with his arms crossed. "Why, of course, she is a lesbian. And she is a model, and a singer. And you are just a dumb boy!" Kamaal's brother laughed. Kamaal didn't know what lesbian meant. He didn't go to school after eighth grade. The teachers considered him a bad company for kids. All he knew was that his friends had used that word to cuss a girl on the internet. That girl used to wear tiny clothes, and always had the crack of her butt on her profile feed. Rage boiled within Kamaal. He couldn't possibly stand the love of his life being insulted. Kamaal reached for the kitchen knife.

One. Two. Three. What did you say? *Four. Five. Six. Seven.* Say that again? *Eight.*

Shanaya Stephens

Nine. Blood. Fresh blood oozed out along with his brother's entrails. He died there, and then in cold blood. Kamaal's mother froze. Silence held them all captive. Kamaal's father was still sound asleep. Kamaal's phone beeped. Someone had commented on her post. It read *"Cut some fat, balloon"*. Rage bubbled up within Kamaal. He wanted to kill that person too. Peony_Pats was everything he wanted in his life.

Oh ah oh aa... They hadn't turn down the fucking music yet. No wonder the people hate the government.

# Kasper, or the father who had failed

Kasper was too old to be on the app, but it didn't stop him. He was seventy-five, and lived long enough to be a paradox. A paradox, he believed was to be something that goes against one's nature. It could be a pretty wide category including a homicidal maniac, to a mummy. He was overtly cool compared to most people his age. He was for a fact, a gamer. That was the easiest paradox he could be. Gamers were the coolest people alive on the planet. That was all one needs to know about them.

Kasper had just ordered a takeout from the local pizza shop. The guy was running late. A paradox right there! Old men do not order pizzas. They die in hospice facility. But not Kasper! It wasn't for Kasper per se. He hardly had the teeth for it. More aptly put, the teeth he had bought weren't that good. He needed to get new ones but didn't really bother. It was hard being a paradox. If you were one, you wouldn't know how to either. So, it was rude, that those plebeians would say something like "Your time is close, grandpa". He was still going stronger, and unlike those meagre menaces; tonight, he had company.

Kasper was made of more secrets than one was allowed. There was this dating app, that he had come to know about from the app. He was going all out to try his luck on that one. She was this girl who lived close by, and had a gamers account. She was hot. He was alone most of them time and didn't see why the lack of teeth must interfere with his awesome libido. He had invited her for dinner. Some pizza, some smooches, and some pretty good time. He had sold himself out.

He was fly, as he would say it. He had made all the pre-date arrangements. It was a nice little touch up on the sheets. He had tried to clean his house but failed miserably, as his back ache set in. His stomach was set in flabby folds, and yet he had managed to lure a girl in. It was an achievement by itself. But then, he hadn't really told the girl what he looked like. He used his son's photo for the profile. That was a sour spot in his life of seventy years.

His son, was a thirty-something man who worked with computers. He had his mother's eyes, and his dad's big dick energy. Or so, his father loved to believe. They had parted ways, soon after his wife passed away. Kasper was old enough now to forget the reason now, but he faintly remembered it... When Kasper was forty-five, he had thought to remarry. His son didn't quite like the idea. They haven't spoken since. He hadn't been married since. Something had been wrong. But then that was most things.

Kasper fixed himself two glasses of wine. One, for himself and one, for when he drops the glass and couldn't bother to come back. He sat by the couch, with the little remote on his side. He had given up on television long ago. Except for Fashion TV, of course.

His phone vibrated on his side. He reached for it, scooped it and turned it on. It was a text from his date. She was running late. This date of his, was a woman in her late twenties. Kasper had seen her boobs in a nude shot. On the app, Kasper was a thirty-two-year-old billionaire who went to Yale.

Shanaya Stephens

That did things to girls that Kasper could never, in real life. They want-only sent him texts, and nude shots. Some of them were terribly hairy, some were clean shaved with a hint of a piercing. If Kasper knew he would land these girls with it, he would have tried it sooner.

At first, this fake profile came off as a spoof. He hadn't really wanted to be on the app, or on the dating app. He just wanted to document his son's life, or whatever little he knew about his son after he left. He just lived at the house across the street. But he left, nonetheless. The App was a hit item amongst the community. Most of the gamers had shifted to it to get more clout. Kasper just wanted to lose the fear of missing out. And now he was way ahead of everyone else. Quite literally.

Kasper had met his date a week before. He was streaming City Walls, and she started being sassy. Unlike most dunderheads, this one seemed to have a mind of her own. Kasper liked that in his girls. Despite his wrinkly skin, and crow's feet, he wasn't a lost cause when it came to romancing the opposite gender. He had them soaking their panties, being loud over voice calls. "Dope shit," they said. This one though... She was in one word 'infatuated' with the idea of him. Kasper was equally amused.

Although he doubted what this possible meet up could lead to, Kasper didn't want to let his date slip away. For one, she was sexy as hell. She had sent him a picture in a bikini, where her tits were barely hidden. The thong hardly left anything to imagination. For a man who hadn't had a taste for a while, that was enough to tempt him in. He wanted to fuck her really bad. If she agrees that is. If not, he would find ways to.

The doorbell rang. A text shot up on the screen. 'I am here', it read. The pizzas hadn't arrived yet. Kasper opened the door. There wasn't anyone standing there. Disappointed, Kasper closed the door. He didn't notice the little rustle behind the bushes. He was too old to catch on things. He went back to his couch. His back was slapped to his cushion.

His phone vibrated again. There were one too many texts. *'Eww. Is that old fat geezer you?', 'I thought you were young. Dude, you are nearly bald!', 'tf is wrong with*

Shanaya Stephens

you'. Kasper didn't know what to respond to. He wasn't bald for sure. Just a little grey.

He just sat there frozen. This wasn't how she talked to him yesterday. Wasn't she the one who told him, 'I would have loved you if you were a worm'? It was getting hard to breathe.

I can explain. He wrote. *There's nothing to explain...*The text came. Kasper's heart dropped. By this time, the doorbell had rung again. The pizzas had arrived. Kasper gave the pizza boy a huge tip, and parted with a thank you. He held the door open, for a while. Outside his porch, two silhouettes stood in the distance.

There was a man. Something about him seemed familiar. And there was a... something that looked like a woman. He wasn't sure if it was one or not. The two of them started to kiss. The pizza boy drove past them. Kasper watched them get handsy, until the femboy had to leave in a haste. The other man, he stood a while longer. His eyes met with Kasper. His throat bobbed but he didn't come. Even if he wanted to. He left in spite. Kasper stood there still. Patrick. He wanted to call onto his son.

A few minutes passed. Kasper's phone buzzed. *'You are such a good kisser. I cannot wait to suck your dick later. I will have you suck mine after...'*

His heart sank. His son wasn't coming back home, then.

Shanaya Stephens

Molly, or the one who couldn't leave

Molly got off her day job at Seb's to serve her customers at her place. She was a high-class call girl. Which was a fancy way to say prostitute! She walked out in a haste with a parka over her shoulders. She had heard someone say it would rain tonight. That was no biggie. At least someone would be wet then, she thought. She was waiting tables all day.

Her place was just around the block. The only reason she worked at Seb's was because it was close. She could go nowhere far in those heels, if not. Especially with a man by her arm. Being a woman calls for drastic measures. You tend to second guess a lot. Molly had done it the entire time she was on this planet. Did it help? No. Was it satisfying? No. Did she want to stop? Also no. Just because something is useless, doesn't mean it should cease to exist. Like, men with opinions about uterus.

Strangers On the Internet

Strangely, that was what would pay off Molly's bills. Men with lots of opinion about uterus. She would find someone who liked really tight pussy. Diabolical, she would say. What could a woman do, when she's poked with a pencil down there? It was something that couldn't be fixed like that.

Tonight, there were no men interested in pleasure. She figured she would just post on the app, and see if someone is interested in her face time services. Those were complementary services that helped keeping the cashflow steady.

She had posted a clean picture of her pussy on the story. There was a link to her Only Fans with it. She had a considerable number of active followers. It helped her with the rent. On days it didn't, she brought her land lord to her bedroom. Thankfully, it wasn't a very public affair. He was her step dad after all. Treachery ran thick in the family. It's not like she had much of a choice. He would have his way with her even if she didn't invite him. It was easier that way.

She had expected the replies to come flooding in. But things didn't seem to go her way. That's just how it was with all things business. You never know what's to come next!

Her apartment smelt like stale minced pies, and cats. On the couch, a tabby slept peacefully. Molly let out a groan. Her legs had already started complaining. Imagine if she had to fuck, with her heels on? She would obviously charge extra. But what if it's him? Well then, she would just think about her mom, and shut the fuck up. Wasn't it obvious? It was all for her mother.

A minute later when she had stripped naked, she hung her head lazily by the mirror. She looked perfect. Her eyes darted on the pink phone cover. She wanted to remove her makeup, but feared for any emergencies. By the time her mind was made, and she went straight to bed, the tabby was awake. No texts still. Years of wearing down, and stress lines were covered with expensive makeup. If only it got easier, somehow. Molly wanted to leave this hell hole. There wasn't much there anyway. Her mother would understand.

Perhaps, it would do her good to go to bed early. She rolled onto her duvet, and then

Strangers On the Internet

her phone buzzed. A text from someone called *DaddyKaspy*.

She was quick to check it. Her services were requested. He had agreed to pay her $1000 for an hour. He was loaded then, she thought. She had promptly forwarded the link to her private streaming platform. *Time to doll up!* She thought.

She had quickly scuttled out her go-to outfit for facetime. Her tits were out, and a cat mask rested loosely on her face. She wore a strawberry pink thong, and touched her make up. She was ready to roll. Hastily, she started streaming on her laptop.

The screen froze for a second before popping up with two camera fields. One displayed her perfect, silicon breasts. The other had the face of a man. He was too old. Perhaps, a little more than seventy. Molly gulped. She wasn't used to such old clients, but then he was paying her a lot.

A notification buzzed in. Someone had transferred two thousand dollars to her account. She pinched her tits, and the man on the screen scrunched his nose.

"Stop all that. I am not in the mood," the man scoffed, and Molly grimaced. Well, that was a first. Most men liked it when she did that. But not the old geezer.

"I want you to listen to me carefully. I am just too lonely. You understand?" The man spoke in what seemed like sobbing whispers, and Molly nodded.

"I am not sure if you are the right person, anyway," he began and Molly nodded silently.

"Do you even talk?" He asked, and she nodded some more.

"Then talk! I need someone to talk to!" He insisted.

"Okay," she offered.

Thirty minutes into the conversation, and she had realised that there was no need to flash her tits. But she was too unbothered to cover up. The man didn't ask her to, so she might even get away with it, she thought.

The man, it turned out lived alone. He had a fallout with his son. That wasn't new now.

Strangers On the Internet

White dudes and daddy issues? Wait, could a dad have daddy issues with his son. No wait, what do they call it then? If there wasn't a term yet, they would probably make one. Americans excelled at making things appear out of nowhere. He probably thinks his son is gay.

"I think my son is gay," he said.

"And?"

There was a minute of silence. Molly groaned when she realised, he was a homophobe. He went about his rant. *God, he was annoying.* Even if he didn't want her to masturbate for him, he was making her want to slap him across the face. He was a pathetic, sore, old loser who has tried to cat fish a girl using his son's profile.

"So, what do you think?" He asked her, letting out a shallow breath. She could pretend that she hadn't heard him and he would keep talking more. But then, he asked her again.

"Like honestly?" She asked, and he nodded.

Shanaya Stephens

"Well, then... I think you should die! You are so fucking pathetic!" Molly bit out. She didn't believe in filters. If someone had told her to die before, she wouldn't be here. For good.

When Molly was sixteen, her mother was dating a man who was twice her age. They had a son together. Dan, they called him. Dan was a sick fuck, who got kicked out because his dad was super pissed when he tried to touch his dick. Dan was weird like that. Molly never really quite understood what his deal was. Only that he was a crackhead. The old geezer faintly resembled Dan's dumbassery.

At dire times like these, Molly loved to reminisce about her sister. Her sister, Nika, was the only one smart enough to leave the wretched city. She wasn't sure why Nika had left. But it turned out that she had found herself a perfect family somewhere in the world. Her sister was a pretty famous influencer now. She had a baby boy last week. Molly was the only one who had written something kind. She had left a subtle, 'He is so beautiful'. It made life less harsh. It made bearing with *DaddyJaspy* easier.

Strangers On the Internet

"I should die? Why, because my son is into those trans-sick fucks?" The old man was not having it. Was he raised a Catholic, and groomed to be an arrogant prick? She wanted to ask, but didn't.

"Why do you even think he is into men?" Molly was fed up.

"My son, Mikhail... He went to Yale. About this big, and ye smart," his rant started all over again. "He is a programmer. In a big tech thingy. I got into gaming because of him. How could he be gay?" How was that even relevant?

Perhaps, DaddyJaspy didn't believe in things like emotions and entities like love. No wonder he was so lonely.

"...Mikhail wanted to try his hacking skills at first. I never encouraged him. He runs a popular page. You know about that Norwegian chick on the app?" He asked, and Molly nodded.

"That's my boy. He photoshopped my wife's pictures to look so beautiful. I cannot look him in the eye for what he has made out of it. He is brilliant, but boy do I hate him!" He spat, and Molly's eyes grew wide.

He tapped his phone for a few minutes, and then pressed it onto the camera. She was a beautiful young woman, with a sweet profile picture. Some Peony_Pats. Wait, it couldn't be!

He possibly wasn't talking about **Peony_Pats**. She was pretty famous, indeed. To think she was not even a living person?

"You are lying old man! There could never be. She has those live streams!" Molly wasn't falling for this shit.

"It's him! He is too good with morphing. Trust me, I would know. I taught him dope shit," he said, and then cringed. "It's not even a livestream... Just something the boys will wank off to," he grumbled.

"That doesn't make him gay, does it?" Molly couldn't wait for the session to end. She certainly felt underpaid.

"Well, he apparently assaulted this guy at a bar. Some immigrant brat who waited tables at a fancy bar. Some Giaret's bar, it's called," the man began.

"They had sex. The boy, the boy he filed charges. Someone got it on camera. I got a call... and I... I didn't know what to do!" The man was barely holding on to his tears. But Molly couldn't care less. This wasn't a part of her job.

"That's not your problem either!" She said, nonchalantly.

"Well, he has been talking to guys. He probably lures them in to sleep and fuck." The old man ran his fingers through his sides.

"No man. Look, like... They got their own life and you don't have shit to do. Mind your business. So, what if your boy's into femboys, boys, or girls?" Molly was not having it.

She would sell herself for sex, but she would never sell her solidarity. She loved queer people. If she could help it, she would have loved a woman. Women didn't hate on most things good. It was diabolical, yes. But that was just one of the saddest things about

Molly amongst others. She was just... straight. If she could help it, she would be with a girl. At least, a girl wouldn't tear her vagina apart. The thought made her shudder.

"You know what, this is crazy. You need to chill the fuck, dude. I am not paid enough for trauma dumping," she barked. She was so done.

"Why would you say that-"

"Just die already dude!" Molly rolled her eyes. "You look like you can do without the over time!" She gasped for air.

The old guy didn't say anything for a long while. It was almost time. Then, Molly saw flabs of skin move in front of the camera. The guy had left his seat. Molly watched amused.

Molly watched the old man get on a bar stool. What she didn't see was the rope that hung loosely from the ceiling. She didn't even notice it until the stool hit the floor, and the man's body levitated over the ground. His legs jerked, and he struggled and then his eyes bobbed out. For what sound like a shriek, Molly had screamed out loud. Her Tabby screeched the pink on the walls. "No, please. He would fuck me for those walls," she cried, as the cat growled.

He had taken her advice after all. Tears ran down her cheeks, as she shut down her laptop. *Fuck, she had killed a man.*

Shanaya Stephens

Acknowledgments

To my beloved friend Kartik, I would forever be obliged. For Tanu and Sahil, I will hold my highest regards. Thank you for doing all that you do for me.

To Ishaaq, who was always there to match my passion for the craft of writing, I would always cherish our conversations. To Dhruv, who told me stories were just words, here are more words to the world!

To my mom, who taught me how to love. To my brother, Noor, who knew how to love without being taught. Thank you for existing.

To Rathnakumar and Sarika, thank you for showing me that the world hasn't lost all its kindness and light.

I love you all.

Kind regards, and love,
Shanaya Stephens

About the author

Shanaya Stephens is an aspiring young adult and teen fiction writer from Vadodara, Gujarat, India. She is author of many poetry collections- 'Vagabond', 'Modern Aphrodite', 'Love Gospel Be thy Queen', 'Small Things', 'The Sandbox', 'Romantica', 'Existential Crisis', 'The Dichotomy of Letting Go', 'Daddy Issues Of a Dirty, Dead, Depressed, Daughter', 'Cherry Fetish', 'Table For One', 'Butterflies, When They Die', and a novel- 'The Bucketlist'.

She is a Wattpad writer, and writes under the username- pea0buttersandwich. Her writings are deeply influenced by slam word artist, and renowned poet - Andrea Gibson, and Neil Hilborn. She is the recipient of Gold Award in Queen's Commonwealth Essay Competition (2022) in Senior Category. She also emerged as the winner of 'Christmas Contest 2.0' organised by the internationally acclaimed, GOI recognised Inkzoid Foundation and received an honourable mention in 'Inkzoid Book Of Records' for her feat.

Shanaya Stephens

Instagram: @shanaya_stephens_ , @pea0buttersandwich Email: stephensshanaya@gmail.com

About the book

'Strangers On the Internet' is a thought-provoking novel that delves into the far-reaching consequences of social media on the lives of everyday individuals. The story intricately weaves together the lives of seven strangers - Krist, Dan, Nika, Archi, Kamaal, Kasper, and Molly - who are connected only by their online presence.

As their stories unfold, the dark side of the internet begins to reveal itself. From the depths of online predation to the devastating effects of cyberbullying, each character's life is forever changed by their virtual interactions.

Through their diverse experiences, 'Strangers on the Internet' raises important questions about the true cost of our online lives. As the characters' paths intersect and collide, the story builds towards a shocking climax that will leave readers questioning the very fabric of our digital society.

Shanaya Stephens

Other Titles By the Author

Vagabond

Love Gospel Be Thy, Queen

Modern Aphrodite

Small Things

Romantica

Sad for the sake of love

The Sandbox

Existential Crisis

The Complete Collection of Poems by Shanaya Stephens

The Bucketlist

The Dichotomy of Letting Go

Daddy Issues of a Dirty Dead, Depressed, Daughter

Cherry Fetish

Table For One

Butterflies, When They Die

Milton Keynes UK
Ingram Content Group UK Ltd.
UKHW040233031224
451863UK00001B/17